ANNIE

The Gorilla
Nanny

For Megan Larkin
J. W.

For the van Os Family, Klub Barbounia members
K. P.

ORCHARD BOOKS
338 Euston Road, London NW1 3BH
Orchard Books Australia
Level 17/207 Kent Street, Sydney, NSW 2000
ISBN 1 84362 155 X (paperback)
First published in Great Britain in 2004
First paperback publication in 2005
Text © Jeanne Willis 2004
Illustrations © Korky Paul 2004
The rights of Jeanne Willis to be identified as the author
and of Korky Paul to be identified as the illustrator of this
work have been asserted by them in accordance with the
Copyright, Designs and Patents Act, 1988.
A CIP catalogue record for this book is available
from the British Library.
1 3 5 7 9 10 8 6 4 2 (paperback)
Printed and bound in China
Orchard Books is a division of Hachette Children's Books

ANNIE
The Gorilla Nanny

Jeanne Willis * Korky Paul

ORCHARD BOOKS

ANNIE

The Gorilla Nanny

Hush now, children! Sit up straight!
Behave yourselves while I relate
My story. Stop that giggling, please,
Or I will have to slap your knees.

I've cared for tougher kids than you.
I trained on monkeys at the zoo.
I took my Nannying degree
In Gibbon and in Chimpanzee.

I've babysat for twin baboons -
I taught them how to eat with spoons,
And how to count from one to ten
Like perfect little gentlemen.

I nursed a young orang-utan.
Well, what a cheeky little man!
He didn't like the look of me
And blew a great big raspberry.

"Nanny won't have that!" I said,
And marched him straight upstairs to bed
Without his teddy or his tea.
(Look, no one makes an ape of me.)

My motto is, "Be firm but fair,"
With all the creatures in my care.
My famous clients don't complain.
I've glowing references from Jane...

...And Tarzan. Their adopted child
Was such a monkey! Running wild!
He wouldn't wash or walk or dress.
I'm not surprised, I must confess.

I blame the parents. Dearie me,
No discipline at all, you see?
They simply swung around on rope.
I swear they'd never heard of soap.

I said to Tarzan, "Wear a shirt!
A pair of trousers wouldn't hurt!
If you wander in the nude,
Your toddler's bound to turn out rude."

I spoke to Jane, I said to her,
"You can't complain of sticky fur,
Or that your boy won't wash his face,
Look at your hair! It's a disgrace."

"Might I suggest a curly perm?"
(I told you I was fair but firm.)
I taught Jane how to clean and cook
And how to read my ape-care book.

Job done, I left their nursery.
They sent a charming card to me:
Dear Annie, thanks to your advice
Our lad is well-behaved and nice.

P.S. Instead of wrestling crocs,
Tarzan washes pants and socks
And helps around the treehouse too!
Love Jane. (P.P.S Thanks to you!)

Their letter came by pigeon post
(So full of praise!). I hate to boast
But in this notelet, at the end,
They asked if I could help a friend.

This friend was not just anyone -
He was the King of Tongistan
And could I meet him Monday night?
(Enclosed: A ticket for my flight.)

I was greeted by the King
And this little hairy thing,
Which kept on jumping up and down
And snatching off his royal crown.

"I bought him for the Queen of France,"
The King said. "There's a Dinner-Dance
In honour of her birthday, she
Is going to be ninety-three!"

The Queen, it seemed, collected apes
Of several different sorts and shapes.
The King had heard that it would thrill her
To receive a young gorilla.

"But it throws coconuts!" he said,
"One hit my servant on the head.
It swears, it scratches and it screeches.
And it spits the stones from peaches!"

"This primate needs some proper training,
Or the Queen will write, complaining
That its manners are precocious
And its attitude's atrocious!"

"Do not fret, your Majesty,"
I curtseyed, "Give the ape to me!
With tough-love and a good routine
I'll have him fit to meet the Queen."

I held it gently by the hand
And said, "Now, dearie, understand
That you must do as I request –
You know that Nanny knows what's best."

"Don't pick your nose, it isn't nice!
Don't scratch your fleas or eat your lice.
Don't stick your bottom in the air
And don't pull faces, strings or hair."

"Don't beat chests, shake hands instead!
Don't suck your toes, it makes them red.
Don't slurp your tea or lick your plate,
Just smile politely, sit and wait."

The little chap was good as gold -
He always did as he was told.
He gave his seat up on the bus
And combed his fur without a fuss.

He learnt to do his ABC
And he recited poetry.
Soon he could dance like Fred Astaire
And always wore clean underwear.

The King was thrilled. (I got a rise.)
The Queen cried, "What a sweet surprise.
What perfect manners! Oh, well done!
He's so much nicer than my son!"

The prince stuck out his tongue and said,
"Naff off, Queenie. When you're dead,
Then I'll be King, make no mistake!"
He sprayed out crumbs of birthday cake.

How wrong he was! For when she died
The people of that country cried,
"Down with the Prince, he'll not be King,
The nasty, rude, ill-mannered thing!"

"Crown our Gorilla, wise and good -
He never spits out bits of food
Or pulls horrid, silly faces
(Or breaks wind in public places)."

They made him King! By his decree
The best bananas would be free.
The children could make nests in trees
And ladies could have hairy knees.

His loyal subjects love him so.
Which really only goes to show
That if you're brought up properly,
You're just as good as royalty.

I'll stay with the King for the rest of his life.
I went to his wedding! (I found him a wife.)
She gave me a job at their palace address...
In charge of the baby Gorilla Princess!

Written by Jeanne Willis * Illustrated by Korky Paul

All priced at £3.99 each

Crazy Jobs are available from all good book shops, or can be ordered direct
from the publisher: Orchard Books, PO BOX 29, Douglas IM99 1BQ
Credit card orders please telephone 01624 836000
or fax 01624 837033 or visit our Internet site: www.wattspub.co.uk
or e-mail: bookshop@enterprise.net for details.

To order please quote title, author and ISBN
and your full name and address.
Cheques and postal orders should be made payable to 'Bookpost plc.'
Postage and packing is FREE within the UK
(overseas customers should add £1.00 per book).
Prices and availability are subject to change.